THE BOY AND THE WHALE

Mordicai Gerstein

ROARING BROOK PRESS  *New York*

For my dear daughter-in-law,
Marina,
With Love

and for
Michael Fishbach and Heather Watrous
of the Great Whale Conservancy

Copyright © 2017 by Mordicai Gerstein
Published by Roaring Brook Press
Roaring Brook Press is a division of Holtzbrinck Publishing Holdings Limited Partnership
175 Fifth Avenue, New York, New York 10010
mackids.com
All rights reserved

Cataloging-in-Publication Data is on file at the Library of Congress
ISBN: 978-1-62672-505-8

Our books may be purchased in bulk for promotional, educational, or business use. Please contact
your local bookseller or the Macmillan Corporate and Premium Sales Department at (800) 221-7945
ext. 5442 or by e-mail at MacmillanSpecialMarkets@macmillan.com.

First edition 2017

Printed in China by RR Donnelley Asia Printing Solutions Ltd.,
Dongguan City, Guangdong Province

1 3 5 7 9 10 8 6 4 2

Every day, I loved to watch the sun rise out of the sea.
One morning I saw something in the water.
Something big.

"That's a whale out there," said Papa. "It looks dead."

We jumped into our panga for a closer look.

"Oh no!" yelled Papa. He cursed the whale
with words I'd never heard him say.
"It's tangled in our net!
Our *only* net!
I hope we can save it!"

"Save the whale, Papa?"
"No, my son, save our net!
The whale is dead."

We dived into the water.

I had never been so close to an animal so huge. Wrapped by the net in a hopeless tangle, the whale must have died unable to move.

I had been tangled
in a net once, too.
I almost drowned.
Papa saved me.

The whale's closed eye was as big as my head.

And then it blinked!
And I had to . . .

. . . BREATHE!

So did the whale.
"*Papa,*" I gasped.
"The whale's *alive!*"
"Just barely," said Papa.
"But our net is *ruined*!
We have no money
for a new one!"

He turned the boat toward the shore.
"Maybe," he said, "we can try to fix
my uncle's old net and borrow it."
"But . . . what about the whale?" I said.
"The whale?" said Papa.

"Maybe we should free it," I said.
"Do you know," said Papa, "how
    difficult and dangerous that would be?"
"But it might live . . ."
"It destroyed our net!" said Papa.
"How will we live?"

" I'm going to see my uncle.
    Forget the whale, and don't do anything foolish."
"Yes, Papa," I said.
    I looked back out to the whale.

I remembered being caught in the net,
feeling helpless, and the awful fear.
What does the whale feel?
It's so big.
I couldn't free it myself.
If I tried, Papa would be
very angry.
I stood there for a long while.

Then I jumped into the panga
and headed for the whale.
I had to try.

I took my fishing knife, hoped the whale wouldn't slap me with its tail, and dived in.

I began to cut away the tough plastic netting.

There was so much of it.
Maybe Papa was right.

I dived and cut and dived again—
If only I didn't have to . . .

...B R E A

T H E !

I was getting tired.
How much longer, I wondered,
could I do this?

Whale? I thought,
Do you have a name?
Mine is Abelardo.

I'm so very sorry about
the net, Whale, but
fishing is how we live.

Do you know I'm trying
my best to save you?
But I don't know
if I can . . . .

When I looked again into the whale's eye,
all I saw was my own reflection.

Don't die, Whale!
I'm doing my best!

But then . . . the net began to drift loose.

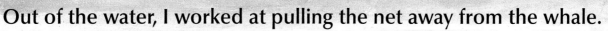

It filled the boat,
but there was still more.

Then I saw the whale move a flipper!

And all at once . . .

. . . the whale was **FREE**!
It sped away from the boat, and I cheered–
"Good-bye, Whale! Good-bye!"

It dived . . .
and disappeared.

It **BURST** out of the water,
leaped into the sky, spun around,
crashed back into the sea . . .
and out again!

The whale slapped its tail and leaped again and again, forward and backward, higher and higher! On and on!

Are you dancing to thank me, Whale?

Or just for the joy of being free?

I watched the whale until it vanished into the sea.
Papa was watching too, waiting on the beach.
I went to face him.

"You actually *did it*?" he said.
"Yes, Papa."
"You *disobeyed* me?"
"Yes, Papa," I said.

"It was incredibly foolish!" said Papa.
"And it was very brave. Now come,
my uncle's net needs fixing."
"Yes, Papa!" I said.